This book belongs to

_____

THE DOVE AWARD SIGNATURE SERIES

Thank You

A VERY SPECIAL STORY FOR CHILDREN

BASED ON THE DOVE AWARD™ SONG BY *Ray Boltz*

STORY WRITTEN BY STEPHEN ELKINS · NARRATED BY RAY BOLTZ

ILLUSTRATED BY ELLIE COLTON

BROADMAN
& HOLMAN
PUBLISHERS

Nashville, Tennessee

With special thanks to Frank Breeden, Bonnie Pritchard, and the Gospel Music Association.
Life is a Great Adventure!

Song performed by The Wonder Kids Choir:
Teri Deel, Emily Elkins, Laurie Evans
Tasha Goddard, Amy Lawrence, Lindsay McAdams,
Lisa Harper, and Emily Walker.
Solo performed by Lindsay McAdams

Arranged and produced by
Stephen Elkins.
CD recorded in a split-track format.

Thank You, written by Ray Boltz © 1988 Gaither Music (ASCAP).
All rights controlled by Gaither Copyright Management.
Used by permission.

Cover design and book layout by Ed Maksimowicz.

A catalog record for this book is available from
the Library of Congress.

*This book is lovingly dedicated
to my wife and best friend, Cindy.
Thank you for the many ways
you have given to the Lord.
I know there is no heart so gracious
and kind as yours on
this side of heaven. I love you.*

I dreamed I went to heaven, and you were there with me.

In my dream I remember holding Mom's hand tightly as we stood before the gates of heaven.

As the gates opened, I saw the most beautiful place I'd ever seen. Inside.....

*We walked upon
the streets of gold
beside the crystal sea.*

THANK YOU

The sea sparkled like diamonds, and God's light shown all around.

Mom always told me that heaven was the eternal home for everyone who believed in Jesus.

We heard the angels singing and someone called your name.

We both turned to see who it was, but all we could hear was the sound of angels singing and harps playing.

Then we heard them call your name again.

11

We turned and saw a young man, and he was smiling as he came. And he said, "Friends, you may not know me now."

THANK YOU

"I was a young boy the last time I saw you."

"It's Stephen Charles," Mom exclaimed, "only he's grown up now."

Stephen was a rowdy boy who attended her Sunday school class.

She didn't think he ever listened to any of the Bible stories she taught.

And then he said, "But wait, you used to teach my Sunday School when I was only eight."

THANK YOU

"I know I misbehaved and caused you a lot of trouble," Stephen said.

"But I was always listening. I loved hearing those wonderful Bible stories you told. You taught me how much Jesus loves me."

15

"And every week you would say a prayer before the class would start. And one day when you said that prayer, I asked Jesus in my heart."

Stephen said he had gone home one Sunday afternoon and told his mom and dad about Jesus' love.

He prayed for his parents just like you had prayed for him. "And look over there," he said. "Because of your prayers, my mom and dad are here in heaven too!"

17

Then another man stood before you and said, "Remember the time a missionary came to your church and his pictures made you cry?"

T H A N K   Y O U

"The missionary lived thousands of miles away in an African village. And you heard about his people who were very poor. They did not have Bibles to read, and the need was great."

Mom, you explained to me that by praying and giving, we were playing a part in helping others hear about God's love.

"*You didn't have much money, but you gave it anyway. Jesus took the gift you gave and that's why I'm here today.*"

THANK YOU

The man explained, "With the gift you gave, I was able to get a Bible in my own language, and I read it every day. Without your gift, I might never have had a chance to read the Bible and learn about Jesus."

One by one they came,
far as the eye could see,
each life somehow touched
by your generosity.

THANK YOU

"How can this be?" Mom said to me. "I don't even know these people. There are so many!" Then I finally understood.

"Mom," I said to her, "when you gave to one person, that person gave to another, and to another. These are the lives you have touched by being a faithful follower of Christ."

Little things that you had done, sacrifices made, unnoticed on this earth, in heaven now proclaimed.

Then you took my hand and said, "When we ask Jesus into our heart, He begins working through us to help others. Look at the lives that have been touched! Yet I know I didn't do any of these things on my own. It was God working through me!"

*And I know
up in heaven, you're not
supposed to cry,
But I am almost sure
there were tears
in your eyes.*

THANK YOU

At that moment we heard the voice of Jesus saying, "Well done My good and faithful servant."

I was so happy to think Jesus was pleased.

26

As Jesus took your hand and you stood before the Lord, He said, "My child look around you, for great is your reward."

I started to tell Jesus how much I loved Him, when suddenly I woke up and realized I'd been dreaming.

I jumped out of bed and ran to Mom.   I couldn't wait to tell her the things I had dreamed.

"Mom, Mom!" I said...

"*Thank you for giving to the Lord.*

I am a life that was changed.

Thank you for giving to the Lord.

I am so glad you gave."

Don't miss the other titles in
the Dove Award™ Signature Series for Children

The Great Adventure
Available Now

*Based on the Dove Award™ Song
by Steven Curtis Chapman*

0-8054-2399-0

Available Soon

God Is in Control

*Based on the Dove Award™ Song
by Twila Paris*

0-8054-2402-4

Testify to Love

*Based on the Dove Award™ Song
by Avalon*

0-8054-2416-4

Available at Christian Bookstores everywhere.